# Kenji and the Cricket

# Kenji
# and the Cricket

## Adele Wiseman

**Illustrated by**
**Shizuye Takashima**

The Porcupine's Quill, Inc.

Canadian Cataloguing in Publication Data

Wiseman, Adele, 1928-
  Kenji and the cricket

ISBN 0-88984-126-8

I. Takashima, Shizuye.   II. Title.

PS8545.I85K4 1988     jC813'.54     C88-094846-9
PZ7.W57Ke 1988

Published by The Porcupine's Quill, Inc., 68 Main Street, Erin,
Ontario N0B 1T0 with the financial assistance of the Canada
Council and the Ontario Arts Council.

Distributed by The University of Toronto Press, 5201 Dufferin
Street, Downsview, Ontario M3H 5T8.

# Kenji and the Cricket

Once there was a little boy called Kenji. He lived
in a big city called Toyko.

Kenji was a war orphan. He had lost his father and his mother.
He had no home to live in and no brothers or sisters to play with.
He was all alone.

All day he wandered the streets of the city, a lonely little boy in
rags, with straight black hair all mussed up, because there was no
one to tell Kenji to comb his hair or wash his face. He had big,
gently tilted black eyes that had a very sad, questioning look, as
though Kenji were asking everyone he looked at, 'Do I belong to
you? Will you be nice to me? Why is there no one to love me? Why
do I have no one to love?'

But people were too busy to pay attention to stray waifs like
Kenji. They only noticed him if he happened to get in their way,
which he did sometimes, particularly when he was trying to be
helpful. And Kenji tried very hard to be helpful, because if he was
helpful to one of the porters in the fishmarket for instance, he
might get a scrap or two of leftover raw fish to eat. If he was
helpful around the vegetable markets he might get bits that had
been trimmed off the greens, or sometimes even a piece of dried
seaweed to chew, which Kenji considered a great delicacy.
Occasionally, even, he would be given a mouthful of rice if one of
the cooks in the small restaurants he begged at happened
to be in a good mood. But more often he was chased away

as a nuisance who was simply in the way.

Kenji often went hungry. He slept where night found him, sometimes in an alley, sometimes under a bridge, sometimes in a doorway, wherever no one happened to chase him away. And yet, no matter where he slept, and even though, on cold or rainy days he was half frozen or soaked through when he awakened in the morning, he was always glad to be awake again. For every morning when he opened his eyes, Kenji thought, 'Maybe it will happen today.' And the very thought would make him glad to be alive and eager to begin the day.

If you asked him what it was that he hoped would happen today Kenji would not be able to tell you. He didn't know. He only felt that one day something good might happen to him. He couldn't even really imagine what it might be, because very few good things had ever happened to him.

Sometimes he imagined that the good thing might be to have all he wanted to eat. Other times, when he was shivering in the rain, he thought the good thing must be to be warm and dry and comfortable all the time. Or else he would think that perhaps best of all would be to have a friend to talk to and play with, so he wouldn't mind being cold and hungry so much. It didn't even have to be a human friend; some other living creature would do. Often he would look up at the sky when he heard the birds sing on a lovely day and wonder how a boy could make friends with the

birds. But in a big city the birds don't often settle on the ground, and when he tried to climb the trees to make friends they flew away.

He hardly ever imagined that the good thing might be for him to find a father and mother. Because Kenji supposed that only the richest and most fortunate children in the world had fathers and mothers, and he could not imagine how a child could get to be so rich and fortunate.

One summer evening, when he was feeling particularly lonely and sad, Kenji found a grassy patch under a tree in the park to sleep on, and was about to roll himself up into a ball and go to sleep, when he heard a very pleasant sound right by his ear. It was a shrill, clear sound, as though some tiny creature was playing an instrument, going 'scrik scrik scrik scrik' with all its might. Kenji was afraid to make a sudden move, lest he should frighten away the little musician, and for a long time he just lay there. It was such a pleasant, comforting sound that Kenji felt the sadness lift gradually away from his heart.

Slowly he turned his head, oh ever so slowly, while the musician fiddled away, paying no attention. There, right beside him, clear in the moonlight, was a handsome, shiny black cricket. He seemed far too busy even to notice Kenji. He was scraping one of his long hind legs against the other, just as a fiddler scrapes his bow across the strings of his fiddle, and from the cricket's hind legs

were coming sounds that to Kenji were every bit as lovely as the notes of a violin are to you and me.

'Perhaps,' thought Kenji, 'perhaps he will be my friend.' And he felt a great longing to have the cricket always close to him, for his very own.

With his heart beating very quickly Kenji moved his hand, very very slowly.

'Please don't move away. Oh please don't jump away,' he prayed. The cricket paid no attention. He scraped and fiddled merrily on in the moonlight. 'I hope I won't hurt him. Oh I hope I don't hurt him,' prayed Kenji as he moved his hand closer and closer.

'All right,' thought Kenji. 'Now!' And very swiftly he cupped his hand over the cricket, as gently as he could. The cricket continued to sing under his hand. Gently, gently, Kenji lifted him up and placed him in his shirt. Miracle of miracles the cricket continued to fiddle even inside Kenji's shirt. And Kenji laughed and laughed, harder than he had ever laughed before, because it did tickle.

Kenji fell asleep with the cricket inside his shirt. The next morning he awoke feeling very stiff because even in his sleep he had been afraid to turn over for fear of squashing the cricket. The first thing he looked for was ... yes, thank goodness, it was still there, lying comfortably asleep on his chest.

Kenji carefully gathered together bits of the greenest grass, stuffed some in his pockets, put some in his shirt with the cricket,

so he shouldn't be hungry, bunched his shirt very carefully to give the cricket plenty of air and to make sure he couldn't slip out of the holes, and started out cheerfully in search of food.

That was a very hungry day for Kenji. Nobody seemed to be interested in his efforts to be helpful. The fish porters motioned him impatiently away. The cooks shooed him off. At the vegetable market he found a few bits of wilted greens and shared them with his cricket. Wherever he went people kept chasing him off, and some even shoved him. Kenji was used to this, but now that he had his cricket to take care of he was worried that his friend might be injured.

But the cricket was not harmed, and towards evening, as a very tired and hungry Kenji wandered about the city, his little friend began again to scrape his legs together. Kenji was so happy to hear the music coming out of his shirt that he almost forgot how hungry he was. A happy smile spread over his face, and he held his arms folded protectively across his chest so the big people who kept bumping into him on the busy streets shouldn't disturb his friend.

As he wandered along, not particularly paying attention to where he was going, it seemed to him suddenly that he was hearing more than one cricket chirruping. He stopped and looked inside his shirt. No, there was still only one cricket there, the same handsome black fellow he had made friends with the night before,

playing merrily away. But there were other insect sounds in the air, a whole chorus of them. Kenji went towards those sounds. He turned a corner.

There on a barrow beside the kerb of the narrow street were piled what seemed like hundreds of little reed cages, very intricately constructed, very very pretty, of all sizes, some decorated with coloured ribbons, some large and some smaller and some very tiny. Some hung down from the cross bars of the barrow and others were simply piled on top of each other. In each cage there was one and sometimes even more than one little singing insect. There were not only crickets there, there were cicadas, there were all kinds of insects, every insect that you've ever heard singing in the grass or in the bushes was there, and all of them were singing away together, so that there was a cloud of music surrounding the barrow so sweet that it took Kenji's breath away. And it seemed to him that when his own cricket heard the others singing it sang even louder, and it seemed to him that his own cricket had the nicest voice of them all.

And what lovely cages! What wouldn't he give to have a pretty little reed cage to put his cricket in. Then he wouldn't have to worry about him being squashed when people shoved him or hit him. Kenji knew that he would never be able to buy such a wonderful cage, but perhaps if he could get close enough to see how they were made he might be able to make one for his cricket.

Kenji came right close up to the barrow and stared and stared at the cages, trying to figure out how someone had made such delicate things. And then he looked at all the insects inside the cages and listened to them singing away, and every now and then he would turn aside to look in his shirt at his own cricket and make sure that none of them was as pretty, or sounded as nice.

He was so busy looking and thinking and listening he didn't realize he was being watched, until suddenly, a man's voice said from quite close by, 'He sounds like a very fine cricket, but why do you keep him stuffed in your shirt? A cricket needs fresh air.'

Kenji looked up into the smiling eyes of the man who had spoken to him. 'I don't have a cage,' he said shyly.

'Then why don't you buy a cage? I sell them very cheap,' said the man.

'I don't have any money,' said Kenji.

'Tell your father to give you some money. I'm sure he'll want you to have a cage for your fine cricket.'

'I don't have a father,' said Kenji.

'What? Well I'm awfully sorry to hear that. A nice looking little boy like you should have a father. Well, tell your mother then. I have a special price for widows.'

'I don't have a mother,' said Kenji.

The man was silent for a moment. 'That's too bad. Where do you live?  Who takes care of you?'

Kenji could hardly understand what he meant. 'Nobody takes care of me. I take care of him,' he said, pointing to the cricket in his shirt. 'I found him last night in the park where I was sleeping.'

'I see,' said the man very softly, 'I see.' And he looked at Kenji in such a sad way that Kenji felt as though he wanted to cry. He didn't know why this man should be so sad.

'Where are you going to sleep tonight?' the man asked him suddenly.

'I don't know,' said Kenji.

'What have you eaten today?' the man asked very sternly, as though he were angry.

'A bit of greens in the market,' said Kenji, wondering why the man sounded angry.

'Did you say you caught that cricket yourself?' asked the man.

Kenji wondered why he was asking him so many questions. He was beginning to be afraid that the man would take his cricket away from him. He started to back away, holding on to his shirt. 'Yes,' he whispered.

'Don't run away. I don't want to hurt you. Do you know, it's not an easy job to find singing insects and catch them without hurting them. You must be a very special kind of boy.'

Kenji could hardly believe his ears. No one had ever told him that he was a special kind of boy before. Hardly anybody had ever even bothered to talk to him much.

'Tell me something,' the man with the kind, smiling eyes said, 'Do you like these cages? Would you like to learn to make them?'

Kenji couldn't even answer. He just nodded his head up and down.

'Then I'll tell you what. How would you like to come home with me? My wife and I have always wanted a little boy of our own. We're not rich but you'll always have a bowlful of rice to fill your belly, and sometimes even a bit of fish and seaweed. I could teach you to make cages and then we'd go out together and catch insects and bring them into town to sell in our cages. Your cricket would have its own special cage. Would you like that?'

Kenji couldn't speak. He just stood and nodded his head and stared at his new father out of his great big black eyes, while in his shirt his heart and his cricket sang and sang.

'Well,' laughed the man, 'if you'll help me pack up the barrow for the night, we'll go home and have some supper and I'll introduce you to your new mother. You know,' he added softly, putting his hand for a moment on Kenji's head and smoothing his hair, 'she's been waiting for you for a long time.'

And Kenji knew now what he too had been waiting for for such a long time.